MORE
FARMYARD TALES

Heather Amery

Illustrated by Stephen Cartwright

Language Consultant: Betty Root
Reading and Language Information Centre
University of Reading, England

There is a little yellow duck to find on every page.

Notes for Parents

The stories in this delightful picture book are ones which your child will want to share with you many times.

All the stories in *Farmyard Tales* have been written in a special way to ensure that young children succeed in their first efforts to read.

To help with that success, first read the whole of one story aloud and talk about the pictures. Then encourage your child to read the short, simpler text at the top of each page and read the longer text at the bottom of the page yourself. This "turn about" reading builds up confidence and children do love joining in. It is a great day when they discover that they can read a whole story for themselves.

Farmyard Tales provides an enjoyable opportunity for parents and children to share the excitement of learning to read.

Betty Root

PIG GETS
LOST

This is Apple Tree Farm.

This is Mrs. Boot, the farmer. She has two children called Poppy and Sam, and a dog called Rusty.

Mrs. Boot has six pigs.

There is a mother pig and five baby pigs. The smallest pig is called Curly. They live in a pen.

Mrs. Boot feeds the pigs every morning.

She takes them two big buckets of food.
But where is Curly? He is not in the pen.

4

She calls Poppy and Sam.

"Curly's gone," she says. "I need your help to find him."

"Where are you, Curly?"

Poppy and Sam call to Curly. "Let's look in the hen run," says Mrs. Boot. But Curly is not there.

"There he is, in the barn."

"He's in the barn," says Sam. "I can just see his tail." They all run into the barn to catch Curly.

"That's not Curly."

"It's only a piece of rope," says Mrs. Boot. "Not Curly's tail." "Where can he be?" says Poppy.

8

"Maybe he's eating the cows' food."

But Curly is not with the cows. "Don't worry," says Mrs. Boot. "We'll soon find him."

"Perhaps he's in the garden."

They look for Curly in the garden, but he is not there. "We'll never find him," says Sam.

"Why is Rusty barking?"

Rusty is standing by a ditch. He barks and barks.
"He's trying to tell us something," says Poppy.

"Rusty has found Curly."

They all look in the ditch. Curly has slipped down into the mud and can't climb out again.

"We'll have to lift him out."

"I'll get into the ditch," says Mrs. Boot. "I'm coming too," says Poppy. "And me," says Sam.

Curly is very muddy.

Mrs. Boot picks Curly up but he struggles. Then he slips back into the mud with a splash.

Now everyone is very muddy.

Sam tries to catch Curly but he falls into the mud.
Mrs. Boot grabs Curly and climbs out of the ditch.

They all climb out of the ditch.

"We all need a good bath," says Mrs. Boot.
"Rusty found Curly. Clever dog," says Sam.

THE HUNGRY DONKEY

This is Apple Tree Farm.

This is Mrs. Boot, the farmer. She has two children called Poppy and Sam, and a dog called Rusty.

There is a donkey on the farm.

The donkey is called Ears. She lives in a field with lots of grass, but she is always hungry.

Ears, the donkey, is going out.

Poppy and Sam catch Ears and take her to the farmyard. Today is the day of the Show.

Ears has a little cart.

They brush her coat, comb her tail and clean her feet. Mrs. Boot puts her into her little cart.

Off they go to the Show.

Poppy and Sam climb up into the little cart. They all go down the lane to the show ground.

"You stay here, Ears."

t the show ground, Mrs. Boot ties Ears to a
fence. "Stay here. We'll be back soon," she says.

Ears gets free.

Ears is hungry and bored with nothing to do.
She pulls and pulls on the rope until she is free.

Ears looks for food.

Ears trots across the field to the show ring.
She sees a bunch of flowers and some fruit.

"That looks good to eat."

She takes a big bite, but the flowers do not taste very nice. A lady screams and Ears is frightened.

26

Ears runs away.

Mrs. Boot, Poppy and Sam and the lady run after her and catch her.

"Naughty donkey," says Sam.

"I'm sorry," Mrs. Boot says to the lady. "Would you like to take Ears into the best donkey competition?"

Ears is very good now.

The lady is called Mrs. Rose. She climbs into the cart. "Come on," she says and shakes the reins.

Ears pulls the cart into the show ring.

She trots in front of the judges. She stops
and goes when Mrs. Rose tells her.

Ears wins a prize.

"Well done," says the judge, giving her a rosette.
He gives Mrs. Rose a prize too. It is a hat.

It is time to go home.

Mrs. Rose waves goodbye. "That was such fun,"
she says. Ears trots home. She has a new hat too.

SCARECROW'S SECRET

This is Apple Tree Farm.

This is Mrs. Boot, the farmer. She has two children called Poppy and Sam, and a dog called Rusty.

Mr. Boot is working in the barn.

"What are you doing, Dad?" asks Sam. "I'm tying lots of straw on these poles," says Mr. Boot.

35

"What is it?"

"You'll soon see," says Dad. "Go and get my old coat from the shed, please. Bring my old hat too."

"It's going to be a scarecrow."

Poppy and Sam come back with the coat and hat.
Then they help Mr. Boot put them on the scarecrow.

"He's just like a nice old man."

"I've got some old gloves for him," says Sam.
"Let's call him Mr. Straw," says Poppy.

"He's finished now."

"Help me carry him, please, Poppy," says
Mr. Boot. "You bring the spade, Sam."

They all go to the cornfield.

Mr. Boot digs a hole in the field. Then he pushes the pole in so that Mr. Straw stands up.

"He does look real."

"I'm sure Mr. Straw will scare off all the birds," says Sam. "Especially the crows," says Poppy.

Mr. Straw is doing a good job.

Every day Mr. Boot, Poppy and Sam look at
Mr. Straw. There are no birds in the cornfield.

"There's Farmer Dray's scarecrow."

"He's no good at all," says Sam. "The birds are eating all the corn and standing on the scarecrow."

"Why is Mr. Straw so good?"

"Sometimes he looks as if he is moving," says Poppy. "His coat goes up and down. It's very odd."

44

"Let's go and look."

"Let's creep up very quietly," says Sam. And they tiptoe across the cornfield to look at Mr. Straw.

"There's something inside his coat."

"It's moving about," says Poppy. "And it's making a funny noise. What is it?" says Sam.

"It's our cat and her kittens."

Carefully they open the coat. There is Whiskers, the cat, and two baby kittens hiding in the straw.

"So that's scarecrow's secret."

"Whiskers is helping Mr. Straw to frighten off the birds," says Poppy. "Clever Mr. Straw," says Sam.

48

TRACTOR
IN TROUBLE

This is Apple Tree Farm.

This is Mrs. Boot, the farmer. She has two children, called Poppy and Sam, and a dog called Rusty.

Ted works on the farm.

He helps Mrs. Boot. Ted looks after the tractor and all the farm machines.

Today it is very windy.

The wind is blowing the trees and it is very cold.
Poppy and Sam play in the barn.

"Where are you going, Ted?"

Ted is driving the tractor out of the yard. "I'm just going to see if the sheep are all right," he says.

Ted stops the tractor by the gate.

He goes into the sheep field. He nails down the roof of the sheep shed to make it safe.

Poppy and Sam hear a terrible crash.

"What's that?" says Sam. "I don't know. Let's go
and look," says Poppy. They run down the field.

"A tree has been blown down."

"It's coming down on Ted's tractor," says Poppy.
"Come on. We must help him," says Sam.

"What are you going to do, Ted?"

Poor Ted is very upset. The tree has scratched his new tractor. He can't even get into the cab.

"Ask Farmer Dray to help."

"I think I can see him on the hill," says Ted.
Poppy and Sam run to ask him.

Soon Farmer Dray comes with his horse.

Farmer Dray has a big, gentle carthorse, called Dolly. They have come to help Ted.

"I'll cut up the tree first."

Farmer Dray starts up his chain saw. Then he cuts off the branches which have fallen on the tractor.

Dolly starts to work.

Farmer Dray ties two ropes to Dolly's harness.
Ted ties the other ends to the big branches.

Dolly pulls and pulls.

She works hard until all the branches are off the
tractor. "Well done, Dolly," says Farmer Dray.

Ted climbs up into the cab.

"Thank you very much, Farmer Dray and Dolly," he says. And they all go back to the farmyard.

The tractor looks a bit of a mess.

Ted finds a brush and paints over all the scratches.
"It will soon be as good as new," he says.

First published by Usborne Publishing Ltd, Usborne House, 83-85 Saffron Hill, London EC1N 8RT Copyright © 1995, 1990 Usborne Publishing Ltd.

The name Usborne and the device are Trade Marks of Usborne Publishing Ltd. All rights reserved. No part of this publication may be reproduced, stored in a retrieval system or transmitted in any form or by any means, electronic, mechanical, photocopying, recording or otherwise without the prior permission of the publisher.
Printed in Italy. UE